Could do even ˄ Better

Could do even Better

MORE SCHOOL REPORTS OF THE GREAT AND THE GOOD

Edited by
Catherine Hurley

SIMON & SCHUSTER

London · New York · Sydney · Toronto · Dublin

First published in Great Britain by Simon & Schuster UK Ltd, 2004
A Viacom Company

Introduction and selection © Catherine Hurley, 2004
Reports © see page 105

1 3 5 7 9 10 8 6 4 2

Simon & Schuster UK Ltd
Africa House
64–78 Kingsway
London WC2B 6AH

www.simonsays.co.uk

Simon & Schuster Australia
Sydney

A CIP catalogue record for this book is available from the British Library

ISBN 0–7432–6384–7

Printed and bound by
Mackays of Chatham, Kent

Contents

Introduction

From Oliver Sacks MD, author of *The Man who Mistook his Wife for a Hat*, in reply to my request for his school reports:

> . . . I am afraid that most of mine have been lost in the abyss of time.
>
> I do not know, in any case, whether they would be too edifying – I remember one, from our Art teacher, who said that I was the worst student she had ever had, and seemed totally incapable of drawing *anything* recognizably (this is still the case); one from my French teacher saying that I had the worst 'ear' for languages he had ever encountered, and that I would never speak or understand French unless I spent a year in France (this too has turned out to be so); on the other hand I got some reports prognosticating a life in science and a life in writing (which, more happily, has also turned out to be the case); and one wise and witty one – which I quoted in *Uncle Tungsten* – saying 'Sacks will go far, unless he goes too far' (going too far has always been a temptation and a danger!).
>
> But, alas! (or perhaps fortunately!) – the originals have gone, and I have only these tatters of memory to remind me.

In compiling this second collection of school reports of the famous, I have come to realize that these 'tatters' are in many ways as significant as the yellowing sheets of paper filed away in parents' attics and sideboards. This volume features recollections from people of what their teachers had to say about them, often in total recall, from such contributors as Jenni Murray, George Melly, Kathy Lette and Fay Weldon. And while it may be tempting to question the word-for-word nature of some of these predictions, it is interesting in itself that this is the version that the great and the good have carried around with them for years, the passage of time in no way lessening the sting of remembered slights.

What I have enjoyed from all of the contributors are their recollections of what it was like to receive these reports, and I have contextualized them wherever possible. Some, for example, apologized in advance for their 'boringly favourable' reports – a phrase used identically by Michael Frayn and Fleur Adcock – and assured me that there were some duff ones some-where that their parents must have thrown out. Peter Hain excuses his exemplary reports as being a result of emigration: 'I had been extremely happy in my secondary school in South Africa, Pretoria Boys High, and coming to an English school in 1966 was a bit of a shock to the system for both me and my younger brother, Tom. Both of us felt almost alien and I overcame that by getting my head down and working as hard as I could.'

As with the first collection I have been struck by how evocative the actual reports can be. Going through the archives at Churchill College Cambridge, for example, and being allowed to handle the very papers that Lady Churchill received from Harrow was a bit of a thrill – much more than it must have been for her, in view of their damning contents: 'A constant trouble to everybody and is always in some scrape or other. He cannot be trusted to behave himself anywhere.' So, wherever possible, I have reproduced a copy of the actual school report itself. In the present climate of computer-generated and anodyne comments from teachers fearful of litigation, as far as I am concerned they are part of the social history of education.

It has also been a pleasure to be put in touch with contributors' parents, who are usually the custodians of the reports. In the case of Michael Foale, Britain's first astronaut, I was delighted to receive a call from his mother. She had contacted him at the space station where he was currently in residence seeking permission for me to ask at The King's School, Canterbury if anyone had any inkling about where he'd end up.

Once again I thank all those who agreed to share their reports, firstly with me and then with a much wider public. As a typical Headteacher might add at the bottom: they have shown themselves to be good sports, which should stand them in good stead in later life.

Explanation of letters
used in reports.

A = Outstanding

B = Good

C = Satisfactory

D = Weak

PUPIL'S REPORT BOOK.

The Pupil is responsible for this book while it is in his or her charge.

Reports will be made twice a year.

This Report Book must be shown at the end of the term to the Parent or Guardian, who will sign in the space provided. It must be returned to the school on the first day of the next term.

When the Pupil leaves school this Report Book will be given to him/her as a permanent record of his/her school career.

(with thanks to Norman Tebbit)

The Reports

We schoolmasters must temper discretion with deceit.

From Evelyn Waugh's *Decline and Fall*

Entertainers

Can't act. Slightly bald. Can dance a little.

> Verdict of Fred Astaire's
> Hollywood screen test

Michael Aspel (1933–)

Television presenter

EMANUEL SCHOOL, WANDSWORTH, JULY 1949

'I'm afraid no documents survive from my schooldays, but I remember clearly the remarks made by my Headmaster, Mr Boome, on my last report.'

Headmaster's comments	*Aspel possesses a certain maturity. Whether it is a superficial maturity, or indeed, a mature superficiality, remains to be seen.*

Joan Bakewell (1933–)

Broadcaster and journalist

STOCKPORT HIGH SCHOOL, 1940s

Needlework	*Joan's stitching could be smaller.*
Progress	*Disappointing. Joan is too easily satisfied by work of mediocre quality. She must bring much greater depth of thought to bear on her work.*
Conduct	*Fairly good. Joan should show more respect for school rules.*

Dora Bryan (1924–)

Actress

MANCHESTER REPERTORY THEATRE SCHOOL OF ACTING, 1939

Report on her Grade I examination in acting:

> *She is alert and obviously possesses a great sense of comedy. In fact, it is clear at this early stage that she is a born comedy actress. Her voice, however, needs considerable attention.*

Simon Callow (1949–)

Actor

LUSAKA BOYS' SCHOOL, ZAMBIA, 1960–62

Poetry & Literature	*Has a very wonderful vocabulary.*
Class teacher's remarks	*He must learn to control his tongue as he has a bad habit of interrupting at inopportune moments.*

Accompanying the report was a note from Simon Callow describing his time at Lusaka Boys' School:

Primitive does not begin to express the standards. On the other hand, nothing has changed – still hopeless at maths; still talk too much; still got a large vocabulary. I note the phrase 'Attends tennis', which very well expresses the level of my involvement with sport.

Lusaka Boys' School

SCHOOL REPORT

P.O. Box 16
LUSAKA
TEL: 83606
. 72416

PERIOD ENDING __2nd December__ ___1960___ STD. __5A__

NAME __Simon Callow__ AGE __11yrs 5 mas__ POSITION __20th__

ATTENDANCE __62__ POSS. ATTENDANCE __191__ NORMAL AGE FOR CLASS __12+__ NO. IN CLASS __29__

	SUBJECT	MARKS GAINED	MARKS POSSIBLE	CLASS AVERAGE	REMARKS
ENGLISH	READING/COMPREHENSION	46✓	50	42	Ex.
	SPELLING & DICTATION	39	40	33	E
	LANGUAGE & TABLES	37	50	32	Ex
	COMPOSITION	41	50	36	Ex - Has a very wonderful vocabulary
	POETRY & LITERATURE	16	30	19	Good considering he has only been in class 1 term
ARITHMETIC	MENTAL & TABLES	9	20	13	
	MECHANICAL	22	40	31	Weakness here. much
	PROBLEMS	46	60	46	consolidation required
	WRITING	17	20	14	Good
SOCIAL	GEOGRAPHY	23	50	36	
	HISTORY	25	50	38	a stout effort
	NATURE STUDY	23	40	33	
	HYGIENE				
	TOTAL	344	500	373	TOTAL = 69
CULTURAL	ART, HANDWORK, MUSIC		Satisfactory		
	DRAMA, YOUNG FARMER'S CLUB				
PHYSICAL	CRICKET, SOCCER, TENNIS,		attends Tennis		
	SWIMMING, ATHLETICS, P.T.				

SIMON CALLOW

Errol Flynn (1909–1959)

Swashbuckling actor

NORTHSHORE SYDNEY GRAMMAR SCHOOL, AUSTRALIA

Errol was the son of an academic, Professor Theodore Flynn. He found it difficult to emulate his father's success. On being expelled, his Headmaster said:

> *Nothing but trouble. I don't know what you need young man, but, whatever it is, this school has not got it. You are expelled, Flynn, for being a disturbing influence on the rest of the scholars.*

John Ford (1895–1973)
Director of classic Westerns

EMERSON GRAMMAR SCHOOL, PORTLAND,
MAINE, 1905–1906

Spelling	*Poor*
Arithmetic	*Poor*
Reading	*Fair*
Language	*Fair*
Geography	*Excellent ('class devoted special attention to capitals, large cities & places of historic interest')*

'John Ford knows what the earth is made of' (Orson Welles)

Robson Green (1964–)

Actor

DUDLEY PRIMARY SCHOOL, GATESHEAD

My reports always read:

> *Robson is easily distracted and easily distracts others.*

Geoff Hamilton (1936–1996)
Much loved television gardener
HERTFORD GRAMMAR SCHOOL, 1947

Geoff and his twin brother, Tony, steamed open the report envelope in the biology lab (as most boys did). The Headmaster's remarks contained the single sentence:

Hamilton is the buffoon of the school

Stanley Kubrick (1928–1999)

American film-maker

PUBLIC SCHOOL 3, THE BRONX, 1934–38
PUBLIC SCHOOL 90, THE BRONX, 1938

During his first term at Public School 3, he missed exactly as many days as he attended – 56. His report cards from Public School 90 show the following ('U' is unsatisfactory):

Personality	*U*
Works and Plays with Others	*U*
Completes Work	*U*
Is Generally Careful	*U*
Respects Rights of Others	*U*
Speaks Clearly	*U*

Only his Cleanliness and Personal Habits were found acceptable.

George Melly (1924–)

Jazzman and *bon viveur*

STOWE, 1939–43

Wrote:

I can find none of my school reports alas, but I remember word for word what the Canadian art master (a comparative lover of mediocre modern painting, but he himself a rather academic artist, in the Augustus John tradition) wrote. His report read as follows:

George has made some progress this year and is certainly very keen on painting and drawing, but whereas he listens with great attention to any praise my wife and I may give him, if we have adverse criticism he simply switches off the engine.

Spike Milligan (1918–2002)

Comedian and writer

WOOLWICH & GREENWICH DAY CONTINUATION SCHOOL, LONDON

On leaving, aged fifteen:

> *He has a very good appearance and is keen, energetic and reliable. He made steady progress in all subjects. I recommend him for employment with complete confidence.*

Little knowing that the employment Spike was headed towards was as a Goon ...

Sheridan Morley (1941–)

Writer, critic, son of the actor Robert Morley

SIZEWELL HALL, SUFFOLK, 1956

Headmaster	*Morley is trying in every sense of the word.*

Jenni Murray (1950–)

Radio presenter of *Woman's Hour*

BARNSLEY HIGH SCHOOL FOR GIRLS

History	*Jennifer tells a good story, but is somewhat cavalier with the facts – could do well in journalism.*

Sting (Gordon Sumner) (1951–)

Singer and songwriter

ST CUTHBERT'S GRAMMAR SCHOOL, NEWCASTLE

His teacher on his achieving 2 per cent in maths:

'Do you know why you got 2 per cent in the maths exam, lad?'
'Er, no.'
'Because you managed to spell your bloody name right.'

Jimmy Tarbuck (1950–)

Comedian

ROSE LANE SECONDARY MODERN, LIVERPOOL, 1950s

Headmaster's report	*Tarbuck courts easy popularity with the juke-box set.*

Jimmy Tarbuck on the Headmaster, E. L. Shepherd, decades later:

I'd have loved him to be there when I got a gong. I'd have liked to come out of Buckingham Palace and said 'Up Yours!'

Sandi Toksvig (1959–)

Comedian and writer

TORMEAD SCHOOL, GUILDFORD, SPRING TERM 1974

Boarder's report	*Sandra's behaviour has been satisfactory, but she is inclined to dramatize some situations.*

Kenneth Williams (1926–1988)

Actor

MANCHESTER STREET JUNIOR SCHOOL, LONDON

One school report of this 'great institution of British entertainment' ended with the words:

> *Quick to grasp the bones of a subject, slow to develop them.*

Writers, Poets and Artists

It is impossible to understand modern English literature unless one realizes that most English writers are rebels against the way they were educated, and it is impossible to understand the strength of the English ruling class until one realizes where it comes from.

W. H. Auden in a 1939 review of Cyril Connolly
for an American audience

Fleur Adcock (1934–)

Poet and translator

WELLINGTON GIRLS' COLLEGE, NEW ZEALAND

A fairly standard girl's school report of its time, revealing not very much of the career to come. What it does reveal is 'my long since discarded first Christian name, which I have gone to great lengths, including a deed poll, to suppress; but I guess I may just have to live with that.'

'I've spent half the morning searching through files of old papers, and eventually succeeded in unearthing one school report. It is the final one and my parents may have kept it because it is so boringly favourable. I don't know what happened to all the others, with the exception of one, which I vividly remember my mother tearing up. It was from the last school I attended in England before we went to New Zealand in 1947. I don't know what it said about my academic work, but my grading for conduct, on a scale of 'Excellent, Very good, Good, Fair, Satisfactory, Unsatisfactory', was 'Satisfactory' – which was of course far from satisfactory. After my mother's spirited response it turned out that none of us knew the exact date on which the following school term began, as she had destroyed the evidence; I therefore had the embarrassing experience of arriving a day early and finding the building deserted.

Wellington Girls' College

REPORT for Half Year Ending 14th December 19 50

NAME of PUPIL ADCOCK, Karean Fleur   FORM VIA.

SUBJECT	NUMBER IN CLASS	CLASS AVERAGE	PUPIL'S ATTAINMENT	REMARKS
English	16	60	79	A very pleasing year's work. K.M.K.
Composition				
Speech Training				
French	12	53	80	An excellent year's work. _?_
Latin	6	55	75 ⎫	Outstanding ability _?_.
~~History~~ German	2	67	85 ⎭	
Geography				
Arithmetic				
Mathematics	8	49	45	Fleur made quite good progress considering
General Science				that she did not give much study time to this
Health Education				subject. AB.

Attendance 205/266   Conduct: Excellent.

General Remarks: A very pleasing report. We congratulate Fleur on being Co-Dux of the School, and on winning the John Lines Memorial prize for English Literature and the Reporters prize for Original Verse. We hope that she has been successful in the University Scholarship Examination.

Form Mistress _____   Principal _?_ Clark

Next Term Begins February 6, 1951.

FLEUR ADCOCK

26

Aubrey Beardsley (1872–1898)

Illustrator and writer

BRIGHTON GRAMMAR SCHOOL

On admission to the school aged twelve, Headmaster Ebenezar Marshall wrote that he:

hesitated to receive a boy whose physique and nervous temperament and special intellectual bent might not profit by the routine of class work and discipline of a large public school.

Some masters saw something in his 'quaint personality' that raised him 'above the level of other boys of his own age'. One recalled how Beardsley was wont to use his 'peculiar dry wit' at his 'academic preceptor's expense'. But biographer Matthew Sturgis writes that one master, when pressed in later years for reminiscences of Beardsley's time at Brighton Grammar School, excused himself as unable to remember anything, remarking peevishly, 'Who was to know he would be great?'

Saul Bellow (1915–)

Nobel Prize-winning novelist

SABIN JUNIOR HIGH SCHOOL, CHICAGO, 1930

Wit and humour abound in him.

Alan Bennett (1934–)

Playwright and diarist

LEEDS MODERN SCHOOL, 1952

Wrote:

> The Latin Master, Mr Seaton, who didn't much care for me, once described me (not to my face) as an autarchic personality. I didn't know what this was and had to look it up (as I suspect he'd had to do) and found it meant self-sufficient. I didn't feel self-sufficient. I didn't feel anything. So I was flattered anyone should ascribe to me any personality at all.

Lord Byron (George Gordon) (1788–1824)
Romantic poet
HARROW, 1801–1805

Byron made his mark at Harrow but not necessarily for his academic prowess. The wife of the Headmaster, Mrs Drury, described him, somewhat cruelly:

> *There goes Birron, straggling up the Hill, like a ship in a storm without a rudder or compass.*

One master lamented his

> *inattention to Business, and his propensity to make others laugh and disregard their Employments as much as himself.*

His

animal spirits and want of Judgement

prompted the Headmaster, Dr Joseph Drury, to suggest that Byron not return for the final term. Byron ignored the suggestion and seems to have made good, as shown by Drury's remarks to Byron's guardian Lord Carlisle:

He has talents, my Lord, which will add lustre to his rank.

Bryon himself wrote later that his 'temper and disposition' changed radically during his last year at Harrow.

Lewis Carroll (Charles Dodgson)

(1832–1898)

Author, creator of *Alice's Adventures in Wonderland*

RICHMOND GRAMMAR SCHOOL

(age twelve) letter from Headmaster, Mr Tate, to his father:

> . . . passed an excellent examination just now in mathematics, exhibiting at times an illustration of that love of precise argument, which seems to him natural, [but he] frequently sets at nought the notions of Vergil or Ovid as to syllabic quantity. He is moreover marvellously ingenious in replacing the ordinary inflexions of nouns and verbs, as detailed in our grammars, by more exact analogies, or convenient forms of his own devising.
>
> You may fairly anticipate for him a bright career . . . You must not entrust your son with a full knowledge of his superiority over other boys. Let him discover this as he proceeds.

Charles stayed at Richmond for a year and a half and 'looked back on his time there with pleasure' and spoke of Mr Tate as his 'kind old schoolmaster'.

In 1846 he went to Rugby and hated it:

During my stay I made I suppose some progress in learning of various kinds, but none of it was done *con amore*, and I spent an incalculable time in writing out impositions ... but I cannot say that I look back upon my life at a Public School with any sensations of pleasure, or that any earthly considerations would induce me to go through my three years again.

Nonetheless, Dodgson seems to have kept these feelings to himself:

Headmaster, Dr A. C. Tait (1849):
... I must not allow your son to leave school without expressing to you the very high opinion I entertain of him ... His mathematical knowledge is great for his age ... His examination for the Divinity prize was one of the most creditable exhibitions I have ever seen. During the whole time of his being in my house, his conduct has been excellent ...

Lord Kenneth Clark (1903–1983)

Author, art historian and Director of the National Gallery

WIXENFORD PREPARATORY SCHOOL, 1910–12

At the end of his last term, his Headmaster's report consisted of three words:

> *A jolly boy.*

Clark then went to Winchester College, where he was unhappy. On hearing the news that Clark had won a scholarship to read history at Oxford, his history teacher, A. T. P. Williams, said: 'I won't deny that I am surprised.'

Daphne du Maurier (1907–1989)
Novelist
OAK HILL PARK SCHOOL, HAMPSTEAD, LONDON, 1917

Class short story competition, teacher Miss Druce:

> *Daphne has written the best story but with the worst handwriting and the worst spelling.*

The prize went to someone called Olive.

Ian Fleming (1909–1964)

Creator of James Bond

Fleming first went to Eton but he was moved to a crammer run by one Colonel William Trevor at Newport Pagnell in Bedfordshire in order to pass the entrance exams for Sandhurst. Colonel Trevor wrote:

He ought to make an excellent Soldier, provided always that the Ladies don't ruin him.

Fleming had to leave Sandhurst when he caught gonorrhoea.

Janet Frame (1924–2004)

New Zealand writer

DUNEDIN TEACHERS' TRAINING COLLEGE,
NEW ZEALAND

	highly intelligent but lacking in social sense . . . [she] seems a lone friendless person always by herself.
Final assessment	*An unusual type; brilliant scholar in languages and a highly intelligent person . . . but temperamentally something of a risk.*

Eerie prescience as the writer, whose autobiographical trilogy was turned into the film *Angel at my Table*, was diagnosed with schizophrenia in 1947 and spent seven years in various psychiatric hospitals undergoing therapy including shock treatment.

Michael Frayn (1933–)

Playwright, novelist

NONSUCH SCHOOL, SURREY, 1941

Age eight:

Michael is a deliberate and careful worker. He reads very well and fairly widely for his age. His general knowledge is well above standard. In his relations with his fellows, he is amiable but does not lack spirit. On the whole, this child shows considerable promise and has, I think, latent abilities that will develop as he grows older.

Nonsuch School,

EWELL EAST, SURREY.

REPORT OF CONDUCT, INDUSTRY AND PROGRESS OF:—

Michael Frayn

Christmas Term, 1941

Age ....

Form I ....

Average age of form ....

	Subject	Term Letter	Class in Exam.	Remarks	
Scripture		A.		Shows much interest in this subject	S.R.
English	Reading	A+		He remembers well all that he reads.	M.H.
	Composition	A+.		Most encouraging.	S.R.
	Dictation	A.		Has made good progress.	S.R.
	Literature				
	Grammar & Language	A		Very good, intelligent work.	J.J.P.
French					
Mathematics	Arithmetic	A+.		Has worked well throughout the term	S.R.
	Algebra				
	Geometry				
History		a.b		Keen and attentive	S.R.
Art				Spirited work.	M.H.
Crafts		A+		Always very good work.	B.C.
Class Singing	Band:-			Improved work. M.T.	
Needlework		A+		Excellent work.	B.C.
General Knowledge		A.		Above the average for his age.	S.R.
Class Elocution					
Games					
Drill		B+		Michael is always attentive and quite capable as a leader. With more effort he can attain good results.	n.n.
WRITING.		B+		.... with more care.	J.J.P.

MICHAEL FRAYN

39

Patricia Highsmith (1921–1995)

Novelist and creator of Tom Ripley

JULIA RICHMAN HIGH SCHOOL, NEW YORK, 1934–38

Teacher	*Shy? Always so very nice to me! Worth watching.*

Patricia Highsmith ricocheted between schools in Austin, Texas and New York. Nonetheless her marks were consistently high. In her final report from the school above she got 90 per cent for English, French and Oral English, 85 in German, 93 in American History, 91 in Hygiene and 85 in Physical Training. Social Training was her weak spot, where she got only 75 per cent. Despite her impressive results, Highsmith did not remember her schooldays fondly, saying that they made her 'feel like a worker ant, without identity, importance, individuality or dignity'.

Eric Hobsbawm (1917–)

Historian

ST MARYLEBONE GRAMMAR SCHOOL, LONDON

Hobsbawm kept a diary for the three years he spent at St Marylebone Grammar School but on winning a Cambridge scholarship in 1936, he decided to end it. Not before, however, as he describes it, 'balancing the accounts, I hoped without sentimentality and self-delusion'. Aged nineteen, he wrote his own report card:

Eric John Ernest Hobsbawm, a tall, angular, dangly, ugly, fair-haired fellow of eighteen and a half, quick on the uptake, with a considerable if superficial stock of general knowledge and a lot of original ideas, general and theoretical. An incorrigible striker of attitudes, which is all the more dangerous and at times effective, as he talks himself into believing in them himself. Not in love and apparently quite successful in sublimating his passions which – not often – find expression in the ecstatic enjoyment of nature and art. Has no sense of morality, thoroughly selfish. Some people find him extremely disagreeable, others likeable, yet others (the majority) just ridiculous. He wants to be a revolutionary but, so far, shows no talent for organization. He wants to be a writer, but without energy and the ability to shape the material. He hasn't got the faith that will move the necessary mountains, only hope. He is vain and conceited. He is a coward. He loves nature deeply. And he forgets the German language.

Kathy Lette
Novelist
SYLVANIA HIGH SCHOOL, NEW SOUTH WALES, *c.* 1974

It is regrettable that Kathryn sees her class role as that of resident entertainment officer.

She shows potential and in some areas her work is outstanding . . . Unfortunately much of her time is spent out standing by the Principal's office because of her classroom high jinks.

Gavin Maxwell (1914–1969)

Bestselling author of *Ring of Bright Water*

STOWE, 1928

His school reports were universally dismal. One master's subject report read:

> *He appears utterly incapable of any form of concentration.*

To his mother:

> *I think if you taught Gavin yourself in Form you would understand what his masters mean when they say that he is lacking in interest and concentration. Gavin's manner suggests the most perfect indifference to what is going on, and he has quite definitely a vein of indolence in him.*

Gavin sank to the bottom of his class, and remained there throughout his Stowe career.

Post schooldays descriptions improved as he was described in *The Times* as 'a man of action who writes like a poet'.

Michael Morpurgo (1943–)
Writer and Children's Laureate (2003–2005)
THE KING'S SCHOOL, CANTERBURY, 1947

English	*After a lazy start he has settled down and worked well.*
History	*He had a rather shaky start . . .*
Latin	*He started well but carelessness lowers the standard of his work.*
Housemaster's report	*. . . This term he has made his mark chiefly and quite definitely on the rugger field . . . I am glad of his interest in the choir and so on, for it would be a pity if all his efforts went into athletics . . .*

Blake Morrison (1950–)

Poet and journalist

ERMYSTED'S GRAMMAR SCHOOL, SKIPTON, YORKSHIRE,
1962–69

First Year Form Tutor	*The unfortunate fall in his form position was due to over-confidence. I think he has learned his lesson this term – namely, that constant effort is the only thing likely to bring worthwhile reward, either at school or later on.*
German	*Most creditable. I must make the point again that his literary appreciation is of a very high order indeed.*
English Literature	*He combines a genuinely sensitive feeling for literature with solid effort and shrewd comment. Thorough in analytic techniques, but he sometimes has trouble in discussion of literary means as opposed to content.*
Geography	*Form position 31/33 – He used to do a lot better than this.*

Pablo Picasso (1881–1973)

Artist

COLEGIO DE SAN RAFAEL, SANTIAGO, 1886

The school was run by a family friend. Pablo ended up spending most of his time following the headmaster's attractive wife around 'like a puppy':

> *If you want your son to learn from my wife how to cook or how she bathes the baby, we can continue with the same conditions, but if you want something more, there will have to be some changes.*

Anthony Powell (1905–2000)

Novelist

ETON COLLEGE, 1919–22

His Housemaster's reports read:

July 1919	*He seems to be very happy here and gets on well with the other boys, no doubt because he is modest and unassuming and unselfish and good-tempered . . . He certainly has character.*
August 1922	*He is a little different from the other boys and I feel that his quiet reserve and dignity may prevent him having any strong influence upon others when he gets to the top of the house. I hope this may not be so but I sometimes fear that they may regard him as superior and coldly critical. That is only an impression that may prove wrong . . . He is the sort of boy that grown up people, as I know, find an attractive companion.*

December 1922	*Anthony has plenty of power even if misdirected at times . . .*
	I don't think he gets on very easily with other boys in the
	house. It may be due to his moodiness, which Mr Bell
	mentions, and a way of speaking which may give offence to
	some because it seems to imply a cold superiority or frame of
	mind too judicial. It may of course be simply due to shyness.

Alexander Pushkin (1799–1837)

Russian poet, novelist, playwright

IMPERIAL TSARSKOE SELO LYCÉE, 1811

Headmaster's report	*Empty-headed and thoughtless. Excellent at French and Drawing, lazy and backward at Arithmetic.*

Teachers' reports	*His reasonable achievement is due more to talent than to diligence.*
	Very lazy, inattentive and badly behaved in the class.
	Empty-headed, frivolous and inclined to temper.

Neil Simon (1927–)

American playwright/screenwriter

UNNAMED HIGH SCHOOL

Maths was a subject in which he was so inept that he once took a test and his paper was returned with a graded score of 'five'. His teacher further humiliated him by writing:

> *A five is worse than a zero. A zero would mean you simply gave up. Didn't answer all the questions and just handed in your paper. But when you get a five, that means you tried and that's all you were capable of.*

She further advised him to avoid a career that required the use of any numbers whatsoever.

Sir Tom Stoppard (1937–)

Playwright

MOUNT HERMON SCHOOL, DARJEELING 1942–46

Report from November 1944 (aged seven):

History	*Good*
Geography	*Very good*
Grammar and Reading	*Good ['Fair' crossed out]*
Writing	*Good*
Arithmetic	*Very Good*
Literature	*Excellent*

continued

POCKLINGTON GRAMMAR SCHOOL, YORKSHIRE, 1951–54

Stoppard left after taking O-levels: 'I left school thoroughly bored by the idea of anything intellectual . . . I'd been totally bored and alienated by everyone from Shakespeare to Dickens besides.'

In the light of Stoppard's later celebrity, the Pocklington school history interpreted his falling out of love with education thus:

Tom Stoppard did not go through the full academic routine; it is the mark of genius not to do the obvious.

Lynne Truss (1955–)

Novelist, journalist and punctuation enthusiast!

THE ORCHARD COUNTY PRIMARY SCHOOL, RICHMOND, SURREY, 1962–63

English	*B+ Very good indeed. A sensible writer – producing good work of a high standard consistently throughout the year. Compositions have been particularly well planned and Lynne has made good use of a lively imagination.*
Conduct	*Very shy. Inclined to fussiness.*

Fay Weldon (1931–)

Novelist

Wrote:

Alas I no longer have my school reports – although I do remember once getting for sewing, 'Good – except buttonholes' and being very cross. I was proud of my buttonholes – if not my hemming.

Charles Wheeler (1923–)

BBC foreign correspondent

CRANBROOK SCHOOL, 1935–40

Geography	*He has done little; but what he did was fair.*
French	*He could do a great deal more than he has done.*
German	*Rarely takes trouble enough to be as good as he could be.*
Spanish	*Maintains an oral acquaintance.*
General Knowledge	*He needs more intellectual humility and to extend his reading.*

This was his last school report and these comments seem not to match up to those of his Housemaster's and Headmaster's on the same report, who sum up his school career more flatteringly:

Housemaster	*This last term of his has considerably stiffened his personal character. The sense of responsibility, so essential for any real enjoyment of life, will – I am sure – be developed further by him . . .*
Headmaster	*He has had a very creditable school career and has developed many qualities which will stand him in good stead. I look forward to his future with confidence and interest.*

Statesmen and Stateswomen

I was allowed to ring the bell for five minutes until everyone was in assembly. It was the beginning of power.

Jeffrey Archer, quoted in the *Daily Telegraph*
16 March 1988

Madeleine Albright (1937–)

First female American Secretary of State (1996–2000)

WELLESLEY COLLEGE, MASSACHUSETTS

From her French teacher, Monsieur François, on her end-of-term paper:

Vos idées sont très bonnes, mais vous avez massacré la grammaire.

(Your ideas are very good, but you massacre the grammar.)

Fidel Castro (1926–)
Cuban leader since 1959
JESUIT COLLEGE IN BELÉN, HAVANA

On leaving, Father Francesco Barbeito:

> *Always Fidel distinguished himself in all the subjects related to letters. He was* excelencia *(in the top ten of the graduating class) and* congregante *(a student who regularly attended prayers and religious activities) . . . He will make law his career, and we do not doubt that he will fill with brilliant pages the book of his life.*

Fidel valued some of his time with the Jesuits, writing that: '. . . the Jesuits certainly influenced me with their strict organization and their discipline and their values. They contributed to my development and influenced my sense of justice.'

He would have been unimpressed with his distinction as a *congregante*, describing the daily mass and sermons of the Jesuit College as 'a form of mental terrorism'.

Michael Collins (1890–1922)

Charismatic commander-in-chief of the Irish Free State Army during the Easter Rising

NATIONAL SCHOOL, LISAVAIRD, 1901

His teacher, Denis Lyons:

> *Exceptionally intelligent in observation and at figures. A certain restlessness in temperament. Character: Good. Able and willing to adjust himself to all circumstances. A good reader. Displays more than a normal interest in things appertaining to the welfare of his country. A youthful, but nevertheless, striking, interest in politics. Coupled with the above is a determination to become an engineer. A good sportsman, though often temperamental.*

The comments on politics and engineering were bracketed with a further shrewd observation:

> *Either one of these could possibly become finalized at maturity.*

Lord Curzon (1859–1925)

British politician and Viceroy of India 1898–1905

ETON, 1872–78

In a letter to Curzon's parents, his Housemaster the Reverend C. Wolley Dod called George Nathaniel:

> *. . . an impertinent brat . . . with a tendency to say silly things and to make silly remarks about the lesson.*

In 1874 Wolley Dod wrote with exasperation that Curzon was now too old to receive 'the best punishment, a whipping' and that he was:

> *. . . often childishly and pertinaciously naughty. He is far too ready with his tongue and however he may be in the wrong he always argues that he is quite right and is very difficult to silence . . . he is apt to be impertinently loud in his self-justification.*

Curzon's biographer, David Gilmour, suggests that much of this master's animosity was aroused by his pupil's clear preference for rival Housemaster Oscar Browning, who described Curzon as 'one of the most brilliantly gifted boys' he had ever come across.

Queen Elizabeth I (1533–1603)
Tutored at home

In December 1539, Thomas Wriothesley, shortly to be appointed Royal Secretary, paid a courtesy call on Elizabeth. Though she was only six years old, she had, he wrote, spoken to him with as much assurance as a woman of forty:

> If she be no more educated than she now appeareth to me, she will prove of no less honour and womanhood, than shall beseem her father's daughter.

For to be her father's daughter was her proudest boast. Back in 1499, when he was eight, Henry had confronted the famous scholar Erasmus. Erasmus was at least as difficult to impress as Wriothesley. But impressed he was. Even twenty years later he recalled the child's poise, precocious learning and (since he was a boy) wicked teasing.

Charles James Fox (1749–1806)
Whig MP
ETON COLLEGE

One of the most colourful figures of 18th-century politics – notorious for the excesses of his private life and rumoured to have conducted an affair with Georgiana, Duchess of Devonshire.

On leaving Eton:

. . . too witty to live there – and a little too wicked

Peter Hain (1950–)
MP for Neath, Leader of the House
EMANUEL SCHOOL, BATTERSEA RISE, 1968

Among the excellent comments made by Hain's teachers, such as:

> *There appears to be no flaw in his record of service to his form and the school*

was this remark from his Philosophy teacher:

> *An editor of Camus spoke of the force of his moral yes & no. I might speak likewise of Hain. Thinks and argues clearly, fervently.*

EMANUEL SCHOOL

Next Term begins 29th April, 1968   Absent _____ whole days

ends 26th July, 1968

AUTUMN TERM   FORM U 6 M & B   of 14   boys   NAME   P.G. Hain
SPRING
SUMMER 19 68   Average age of Form 18.1   Age at end of Term 18.1

Subject	†Attainment	*Effort	Remarks
Pure Mathematics	2	A	He has continued to work very well and is improving his standard. His work on past papers is thorough and a good preparation for the S.M. Examination. EHH
Applied Mathematics	2	A	His standard has continued to improve and he is acquiring a good grasp of the principles and methods of this subject. CBS
Physics set I.	3	B	Very good, careful, painstaking work at all times. KWL.
Recent European History	1	A.	an excellent term's work.
Philosophy Option	1	A	An editor of Cygnus of the of the force of his original ... On I think ... and argues clearly, fervently. I ...
English			He is interested and prepared to discuss. D.W.E.

† Grades 1, 2, 3, 4, 5, 6, 7, 8, 9, in descending order of merit, are given for the boy's academic attainment judged in terms of the established standards of this School.

* Grades A, B, C, D, E, in descending order of merit, are given for "effort," the boy's willingness to learn and application to his work.

PETER HAIN

Lord Douglas Hurd (1930–)

Foreign Minister in Margaret Thatcher's government (1989–95)

CRAY COURT KINDERGARTEN, MARLBOROUGH, WILTSHIRE

At age six:

> *Why is he so nervous? Particularly when his mother is away.*
>
> *Douglas finds a good deal of his work easy, which is lucky, because he does not persevere when he meets a difficulty. He asks for guidance on silly little points connected with his work and so must be urged to be more self reliant.*

A year later:

> *A very good term. Douglas does not fuss now, and looks after Julian* [his brother] *very well on Fridays.*

On Handwork – Raffia and Woollen Ball:

Douglas should be made to use his hands – nothing finicky or he will be discouraged.

Benito Mussolini (1883–1945)
Fascist dictator of Italy (1925–43)
L'ISTITUTO SALESIANO, FAENZA, 1894

Il Duce was not happy at this school and his time there ended badly, when he was expelled after he stabbed another pupil in the hand after a fight. His report described him as possessing a

> *. . . lively intelligence, an impressive memory, but of a totally disorganised kind.*
> *. . . passionate and unruly. He opposes every order and discipline of the college.*
> *Nothing fulfils him: in a group of people he feels sad and lonely. He wants to be*
> *alone.*

Mussolini was happier at his next school and, despite another stabbing incident, passed his final exam in 1910 with distinction, receiving 132 out of a possible 150 marks. His best subjects were history, Italian, literature and choral singing.

Steven Norris (1945–)

Conservative politician

LIVERPOOL INSTITUTE HIGH SCHOOL FOR BOYS, 1950s

I seriously doubt this boy's ability to get into the sixth form.

Clare Short (1946–)

Labour politician, former Cabinet Minister

ST PAUL'S GRAMMAR SCHOOL, 1950s

Clare is not using her ability. She is talkative and often very inattentive.

Good but far too talkative.

Lord Norman Tebbit (1931–)
Minister in Margaret Thatcher's government
EDMONTON COUNTY GRAMMAR SCHOOL, 1942–47

Norman Tebbit wrote:

> Thank you for your letter about *Could Do Better*. I found that said of me at school and I'm afraid it is true. I could have done better.
>   Never mind. I will keep trying in my own way.

Form Master	*A contrast between term and exam positions indicates that with a little more effort Tebbitt [sic] could hold a position high up in the class. Please make this effort – ability without real effort is not very creditable.*
Physical exercises	*Good. Posture bad.* *Tries, but room for improvement.* *Fair, seldom takes part.* *Always excuses, must commence next term.* *Fair, lacks keenness, could do better.*

Nonetheless:

COUNTY COUNCIL OF MIDDLESEX.
BOROUGH OF EDMONTON
EDUCATION COMMITTEE.

————◦◦◦◦◦————

EDMONTON COUNTY SCHOOL,
CAMBRIDGE ROAD,
ENFIELD, MIDDX.

HEADMASTER:
H. B. CHAMPION, B.Sc.

TEL.: LABURNUM 3158.

11th July, 1947.

NORMAN TEBBITT.

N. Tebbitt, who has been with us for five years, has academic ability well above the average. He has been in the Specialist Science Form for three years; but he is strong at all subjects.

He has taken a full and loyal part in school life. He has been particularly keen on the Debating Society, and he is probably the best extempore speaker in the school. He has also made his mark on the elected School Council.

He is a mature, self-possessed boy who has worked steadily throughout the school course and he should do very well.

HEAD MASTER

Queen Victoria (1819–1901)

TUTORED FROM THE AGE OF FOUR

Home tutor, Reverend George Davys, Fellow of Christ's College, Cambridge:

> She was not very good at Latin, and piano lessons were often a trial. Once, when told that there was 'no royal road to success in music' and that she must practise like everyone else, she banged shut the lid of the instrument with the defiant words:
>
> 'There, you see, there is no must about it!'

Harold Wilson (1916–1995)
Labour Prime Minister 1964–70; 1974–76
ROYDS HALL GRAMMAR SCHOOL, HUDDERSFIELD, 1927

According to his Headmaster, he showed no early signs of academic brilliance and his record was:

no better than that of the average intelligent lad

but

He was alert. He was cheerful. He had an enquiring mind. He was determined to make a success of anything he tackled; and, above all, he was popular with his colleagues.

History was his favourite subject. Told to write an essay on the position he would like to achieve in twenty-five years, he chose Chancellor of the Exchequer and gave the details of his first budget – it included a tax on gramophones as being a luxury enjoyed only by the idle rich.

The school magazine, the *Roydsian*, described his first effort at debating as having:

a brilliant opening sentence

It proved to be the closing sentence as well since he abruptly sat down as soon as it had been delivered. Excessive brevity, however, was not for long to be a feature of Wilson's oratory . . .

Inventors, Explorers, Innovators and Other Movers and Shakers

An inventor is simply a fellow who doesn't take his education too seriously.

> Charles Franklin Kettering (1876–1958)
> American inventor of the first electrical
> ignition system, one of the 140 patents
> he held during his lifetime.

Dr Mary Archer (1944–)

Scientist and wife of Jeffrey

ST CHRISTOPHER'S SCHOOL, EPSOM, SURREY, 1950

At age six:

> *Gymnastics – Mary works well. She must learn not to mind if she cannot always be a leader.*

Anthony Blunt (1907–1983)

Keeper of the Queen's pictures

MARLBOROUGH

The following appeared in the *Marlburian*, in a review of a school magazine edited by Blunt. The review was written by Blunt's favourite teacher.

> *Fire always burns if one approaches too close – however much one insists that it doesn't.*

On speech day, Turner, another teacher well disposed to Blunt, said:

> *Blunt and some others may go image-breaking, but that is no bad thing so long as the hammer is swung fair and square, and at the image and not at the heads of rival worshippers.*

Richard Dawkins (1941–)

Professor of Zoology, author of *The Selfish Gene* and *The Blind Watchmaker*

EAGLE SCHOOL, SOUTHERN RHODESIA (now Zimbabwe)

Report by Matron on his first term at boarding school, aged seven:

> *Dawkins has only three speeds: slow, very slow, and stop.*

Then, Chafyn Grove School, Salisbury (England), aged eight:

French	*Plenty of ability – a good pronunciation and a wonderful facility in escaping work.*
Latin	*He has made steady progress but unfortunately when using ink his written work becomes very untidy.*

Mathematics	*He works very well but I am not always able to read his work. He must learn that ink is for writing, not washing, purposes . . .*
Headmaster's Report	*He has produced some good work and well deserves his prize. A very inky little boy at the moment, which is apt to spoil his work.*

James Dyson (1947–)
Maverick inventor
GRESHAMS, NORFOLK

James Dyson's father was classics master at Greshams. After he died, James stayed at the school (through the generosity of the Headmaster) but his academic success didn't mirror that of his father. Unlike his contemporaries – who were all going off to university or to do VSO – Dyson chose to go to art school. His mother received the following letter from the Headmaster, Logie Bruce Lockhart:

Dear Mary

We shall be sorry to part with James. I cannot believe that he is not really quite intelligent, and I expect it will be brought out somehow somewhere.

Yours sincerely Logie BL.

Dyson wrote back thanking him for his encouragement and received the following reply:

Dear James

It was very civil of you to offer your thanks for the little we have done. The academic side, although we have to pretend it is important, matters comparatively little. You will do all the better for not having masses of tiresome degrees full of booklearning hanging round your neck. Good luck at Art School.

Yours sincerely Logie Bruce Lockhart.

Rio Ferdinand (1978–)
England and Manchester United footballer

Rio had a trial for a place in the England Under-15 side and got this report:

One-paced. Lacks concentration. Good attitude. Mark: B

Major Ronald Ferguson (1931–2003)

Polo-playing father of the Duchess of York

MISS DENNISON'S

Major Ferguson writes:

> It would seem that mothers then were just as competitive as they are now. One of them asked my mother one day, 'Have you had this term's report? What did it say about Ronald?'
>
> 'Trying,' Mother said. 'I think that's marvellous because he is so lazy.'
>
> Next term the same mother was upset because her son had received a bad report. 'Have you had yours? What did it say?' she asked.
>
> My mother still recalls her reply: 'It said, "Very trying."'

Michael Foale (1957–)

Britain's first astronaut

THE KING'S SCHOOL, CANTERBURY, 1973

Aged sixteen, summer term:

Astronomy	*He has occasionally failed to see the most elementary point, but he has worked enthusiastically and should have acquired sufficient knowledge to satisfy the examiner.*

W.G. Grace (1848–1915)

Greatest ever cricketer

RUDGEWAY HOUSE SCHOOL

> *a steady working lad, accurate at mathematics, with no mischief in him.*

A biography published in 1919 – *The Memorial Biography of Dr W.G. Grace* by W. Methven Brownlee – notes that his greatest achievement at school was becoming marbles champion:

'. . . on one occasion clearing out the school'.

W.G. left Rudgeway House aged fourteen.

Professor Susan Greenfield (1950–)
Scientist, CBE and writer
CAVENDISH PRIMARY SCHOOL, 1960

At the age of nine years and five months, Susan Greenfield was top of her class of thirty-one pupils, getting straight-As and A+. Said her teacher:

> *A girl of very great promise – very much alive and continuing to make excellent progress. Well done!*

According to her mother, this was the only one of Susan's reports that was kept, 'although all her reports were very, very good'.

Trevor Huddleston (1913–1998)

Anglican monk and leader of the Anti-Apartheid Movement.

LANCING COLLEGE

Man who coached him for a scholarship to Lancing, the leading High Anglican public school:

> *not a scholar, just an average, charming, friendly prep-school boy*

and:

Master of the Sixth Form	*a good citizen, no flyer*

Brian Johnston (1912–1994)

Cricket commentator

TEMPLE GROVE PREP SCHOOL, 1920s

Like many prep schools of the time, Temple Grove had a Cadet Corps, run by Chief Petty Officer Crease. Colonel Mitford, the CO, reported that:

> *Platoon Drill under Sergeant Johnston and Sergeant Hearn was very good.*

According to the school magazine, he kept wicket for the First XI in his two final years,

> *very successfully*

but his batting was more suspect:

An eccentric bat and a bad judge of a run.

In his final year, he was praised for his:

never failing keenness

Derek Malcolm (1932–)
Film critic
SUMMERFIELDS SCHOOL, OXFORD

Teacher's report	*Bloody idle swine!*

(Derek Malcolm's father threatened to horsewhip him – no idle threat as he was later charged with murdering his wife's lover.)

At Eton College:

Housemaster's report	*Derek is very unlikely to benefit much from university, even if he was lucky enough to get in, which I'm afraid I doubt. Might I suggest the Army, or possibly farming? Neither of these might prove too difficult for him.*

Mary Warnock (1924–)

Philosopher, Life Peer, Principal of Hertford College, Oxford, and Vice Chancellor of Oxford University

ST SWITHUN'S, WINCHESTER, 1937

She was considered quite bright, but as the youngest in her form, she never performed very well. She was once told by her Headmistress that she:

> *prostituted her intellect*

The Last Word

Sir Georg Solti (1912–1997)

Celebrated conductor

FRANZ LISZT ACADEMY, BUDAPEST

When he was seventeen, one of the examiners told him:

We're passing you as a favour both to you and ourselves. We don't want you to come back.

Acknowledgements & Sources

Thanks to Judith Hannam for all the research she did which came at exactly the right time, and also to Andrew Nickolds and Ingrid Connell for their help. I'm grateful also to Cassandra Campbell at Simon & Schuster for her patient support and to Helen Gummer, who kicked the whole thing off.

The following list gives in order of appearance in the book the sources of each entry with copyright details where appropriate. I have omitted all entries where the source is the subject. The editor and publishers are grateful to all copyright holders for permission to reproduce material under their control. It has not proved possible to trace the copyright holder of every report and we would be grateful to be notified of any corrections, which will be incorporated in reprints in future editions of this volume.

Dora Bryan's report from *According to Dora* by Dora Bryan, Hodder &

Stoughton, 1996; Errol Flynn's from *My Wicked, Wicked Ways* by Errol Flynn, William Heinemann, 1960; John Ford's from *Searching for John Ford* by Joseph McBride, St Martin's Press, 2001; Janet Frame's from *Wrestling with the Angel: A Life of Janet Frame* by Michael King, Picador, 2002; Robson Green's from *Just the Beginning* by Robson Green, Boxtree, 1998; Geoff Hamilton's from *My Brother Geoff* by Tony Hamilton, Headline, 2001; Stanley Kubrick's from *Kubrick: A Biography* by John Baxter, HarperCollins, 1997; Spike Milligan's from *Spike: The Biography* by Humphrey Carpenter, Hodder & Stoughton, 2003; Sting's from *Broken Music* by Sting, Simon & Schuster, 2003, courtesy the author; Kenneth Williams' from *Just Williams: An Autobiography*, J. M. Dent & Sons, 1985; Aubrey Beardsley's from *Aubrey Beardsley* by Matthew Sturgis, HarperCollins, 1998; Saul Bellow's from *Saul Bellow* by James Atlas, Faber & Faber, 2000; Byron's from *Byron: Life & Legend* by Fiona MacCarthy, John Murray, 2002 and *Lord Byron at Harrow School* by Paul Elledge, Johns Hopkins University Press, 2000; Lewis Carroll's from *Lewis Carroll* by Derek Hudson, Constable, 1954 (sourced to *The Life and Letters of Lewis Carroll* by Stuart Dodgson Collingwood, Fisher Unwin, 1898); Kenneth Clarke's from *Another Part of the Wood: A Self Portrait*, John Murray, 1974; Daphne du Maurier's from *Daphne: A Portrait of Daphne du Maurier* by Judith Cook, Bantam Press, 1991, courtesy Jim

Reynolds Associates; Ian Fleming's from *Ian Fleming* by Andrew Lycett, Weidenfeld & Nicolson, 1995; Patricia Highsmith's from *Beautiful Shadow: A Life of Patricia Highsmith* by Andrew Wilson, Bloomsbury, 2003; Eric Hobsbawm's from *Interesting Times* by Eric Hobsbawm, Allen Lane, 2002, with permission of the author; Gavin Maxwell's from *Gavin Maxwell: A Life* by Douglas Botting, HarperCollins, 1993, courtesy Johnson & Alcock Ltd; Picasso's from *Picasso: Creator and Destroyer* by Arianna Stassinopoulos Huffington, Weidenfeld & Nicolson, 1988, courtesy PFD; Anthony Powell's from *Infants of the Spring* by Anthony Powell, Heinemann, 1976; Alexander Pushkin's from *Pushkin* by T. J. Binyon, HarperCollins, 2002; Neil Simon's from *Rewrites: A Memoir*, Simon & Schuster, 1996; Georg Solti's from *A Memoir* by Georg Solti, Chatto & Windus, 1997; Madeleine Albright's from *Madam Secretary: A Memoir*, Macmillan, 2003; Fidel Castro's from *Fidel Castro* by Volker Skierka, Polity Press, 2004; Michael Collins' from *A Life* by James Mackay, Mainstream Publishing, 1996; Curzon's from *Curzon* by David Gilmour, John Murray, 1994; Elizabeth I's from *Elizabeth* by David Starkey, Chatto & Windus, 2000; Charles James Fox's from *Charles James Fox* by L. G. Mitchell, Oxford University Press, 1992; Mussolini's from *A Life* by Nicholas Farrell, Weidenfeld & Nicolson, 2003; Queen Victoria's from *Queen Victoria: A Personal History* by Christopher Hibbert, HarperCollins,

2000; Harold Wilson's from *The Authorised Life* by Philip Ziegler, Weidenfeld & Nicolson, 1993; Anthony Blunt's from *Anthony Blunt: His Lives* by Miranda Carter, Macmillan, 2001; James Dyson's from *Against the Odds: An Autobiography*, Orion Business Books, 1998; Rio Ferdinand's reprinted from *The Guardian*, 20 December 2003; Ronald Ferguson's from *The Galloping Major: My Life in Singular Times*, Macmillan, 1994; W. G. Grace's from *WG* by Robert Low, Richard Cohen Books, 1997; Trevor Huddleston's from *A Life* by Robin Denniston, Macmillan, 1999; Brian Johnston's from *The Authorised Biography* by Tim Heald, Methuen, 1995; Derek Malcolm's from *Family Secrets*, Hutchinson, 2003; Mary Warnock's from *People and Places: A Memoir*, Duckworth, 2000; Jimmy Tarbuck's heard on *Desert Island Discs*, 11 January 2004.

The Dyslexia Institute

What is dyslexia?

Dyslexia causes difficulties in learning to read, write and spell. Short-term memory, mathematics, concentration, personal organisation and sequencing may also be affected.

Dyslexia usually arises from a weakness in the processing of language-based information. Biological in origin, it tends to run in families, but environmental factors also contribute.

Dyslexia can occur at any level of intellectual ability. It is not the result of poor motivation, emotional disturbance, sensory impairment or lack of opportunities, but it may occur alongside any of these.

The effects of dyslexia can be largely overcome by skilled specialist teaching and the use of compensatory strategies.

Dyslexia is the most common of the learning difficulties, affecting 10 per cent of the UK population and up to 4 per cent have severe dyslexia, including some 375,000 schoolchildren. It can affect anyone of any age.

Dyslexia is complex due to variation in the number, type and severity of its associated difficulties. The manifestation of the difficulties dyslexia causes are influenced by the individual's personality and intelligence, their parents, schooling and/or social and economic background. All these factors make dyslexia a very individual condition.

The Dyslexia Institute

Dyslexia can affect an individual's performance, have serious social implications and cause behavioural problems as a result of continuous underachievement. It is for this reason that the Dyslexia Institute (DI) is dedicated to ensuring that as many individuals with dyslexia are identified and helped as possible.

The DI is an educational charity, founded in 1972. It has grown to become the only national dyslexia teaching organization in the world. The Institute carries out assessments for children and adults who may have dyslexia, provides specialist tuition for dyslexic people of all ages, trains specialist teachers, develops teaching materials and conducts research to ensure best provision and support for dyslexic people.

The DI employs over 220 specialist teachers, its own chartered psychologists, speech and language therapists, and support staff. In addition, some 70 educational psychologists work for the DI on a consultancy basis. The Institute has 27 main Centres and over 140 smaller teaching units throughout the country but it is continuously working to increase its outreach.

Could Do Better

'Could do better', is a term that some individuals who are dyslexic will remember from their school days. However, many dyslexic people are often artistic, creative, original, lateral thinkers and as a result very often excel in careers such as design, engineering, architecture, IT or medicine. There are many dyslexic individuals who do very well in their chosen professions but the DI strives to ensure that all people with dyslexia have an equal opportunity to reach their full potential.

The Dyslexia Institute would like to thank Catherine Hurley and Simon & Schuster for their continued support. The royalties generated to date have been used to improve the support that the Institute's Centres are able to offer to children and adults who are dyslexic.

For More Information:

Address: The Dyslexia Institute, Park House, Wick Road,
                  Egham, Surrey, TW20 0HH
Tel: 01784 222300
E-Mail: info@dyslexia-inst.org.uk

Please visit the DI's website at www.dyslexia-inst.org.uk

Index

Greenfield, Susan	91	Norris, Steven	71
Hain, Peter	66	Picasso, Pablo	46
Hamilton, Geoff	13	Powell, Anthony	47
Highsmith, Patricia	40	Pushkin, Alexander	49
Hobsbawm, Eric	41	Short, Clare	72
Huddleston, Trevor	92	Simon, Neil	50
Hurd, Lord Douglas	68	Solti, Sir Georg	99
Johnston, Brian	93	Sting (Sumner, Gordon)	19
Kubrick, Stanley	14	Stoppard, Sir Tom	51
Lette, Kathy	42	Tarbuck, Jimmy	20
Malcolm, Derek	95	Tebbit, Lord Norman	73
Maxwell, Gavin	43	Toksvig, Sandi	21
Melly, George	15	Truss, Lynne	53
Milligan, Spike	16	Victoria, Queen	75
Morley, Sheridan	17	Warnock, Mary	96
Morpurgo, Michael	44	Weldon, Fay	54
Morrison, Blake	45	Wheeler, Charles	55
Murray, Jenni	18	Williams, Kenneth	22
Mussolini, Benito	70	Wilson, Harold	76

POCKET
BOOKS

COULD DO BETTER
School Reports of the Great and the Good
Edited by Catherine Hurley

From Winston Churchill to Charlotte Church, COULD DO BETTER is a selection of the school reports of the great, the good (and the fictional), and a backward look at history's high achievers. Funny acerbic, often startingly accurate, sometimes wildly inaccurate, this first collection celebrates what is now a dying art – the one chance for tormented frazzled teachers to have the last word:

RICHARD BRIERS:
'It would seem that Briers thinks he is running the school and not me.
If this attitude persists, one of us will have to leave.'

ROBERT GRAVES:
'Well, goodbye Graves, and remember that your best friend
is the waste-paper basket.'

JILLY COOPER:
'Jilly has set herself an extremely low standard
which she has failed to maintain.'

ISBN 0 7434 5025 6
PRICE £5.99